Parke Godwin

George William Curtis

A commemorative address delivered before the Century Association, New

York, December I7, 1892

Parke Godwin

George William Curtis
A commemorative address delivered before the Century Association, New York, December 17, 1892

ISBN/EAN: 9783337419158

Printed in Europe, USA, Canada, Australia, Japan

Cover: Foto ©Andreas Hilbeck / pixelio.de

More available books at **www.hansebooks.com**

GEORGE WILLIAM CURTIS

A Commemorative Address

DELIVERED BEFORE

THE CENTURY ASSOCIATION, NEW YORK

December 17, 1892

BY

PARKE GODWIN

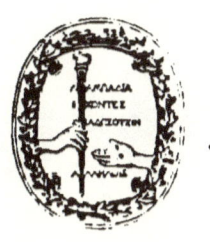

NEW YORK

HARPER & BROTHERS PUBLISHERS

1893

" Oh, weep for Adonais, though our tears
  Thaw not the frost that binds so dear a head."

SHELLEY.

" The idea of thy life shall sweetly creep
  Into my study of imagination :
  And every lovely organ of thy life
  Shall come apparelled in more precious habit,
  More moving delicate and full of life,
  Into the eye and prospect of my soul,
  Than when thou liv'st indeed."

SHAKESPEARE.

" Green be the turf above thee,
  Friend of my better days !
  None knew thee but to love thee,
  Nor named thee but to praise."

HALLECK.

GEORGE WILLIAM CURTIS

We are brought together to-night to do honor to the memory of a fellow-member who had long prized and adorned our association—whom many of you knew, and knew only to admire and love—George William Curtis. He died on the 31st of August last—the closing day of a brilliant summer—at his home near the shore of the sea whose moans are now his requiem.

It is a sorrowful task for me to utter the memorial words you require, because, although somewhat younger than myself, he was one of my earliest as well as latest friends, with whom I was for some time associated in earnest political and literary work, whom I never approached or even thought of without a glow of affection, and whose loss has filled my eyes, as it

I

has those of many others, with unavailing tears; and yet, so vivid a personality was he to me that, knowing him gone, I cannot, in the phrase of one of our older poets, " make him dead." It is almost impossible for me to think that the manly form so full of activity, and the attractive face always aglow with light and sweetness, are motionless forever; that the voice which music itself attuned to the expression of every noble and tender human sentiment is still, and so still; that the busy brain which forged for us the solid bolts of reason and built the beautiful fabrics of fancy has ceased to work; and that the large, honest, and loving heart will beat no more.

In complying with your request I shall offer you no biography of Mr. Curtis, for which the time allotted to my task would be inadequate, and I can only refer to those leading events of his life which will enable you to appreciate best his character and services as a writer, a speaker, a citizen, and a man.

Mr. Curtis, although a resident of New York since his fifteenth year, was a native of New England. He was born on the 24th of February, 1824—within that decade which saw the first gleams of a permanent American literature in the writings of Dana, Irving, Bryant, Cooper, Halleck, and the yet unnoted Poe—at Providence, Rhode Island — a State where Roger Williams had early planted the seeds of a true spiritual liberty, and Bishop Berkeley, the friend of Addison, Pope, and Steele, and the founder of an ideal philosophy, had left the traditions of his presence.

His ancestors on both sides were of the Puritan stock—not particularly distinguished as I find, save that his mother's father, James Burrill, Jr., was a Chief Justice of the State and a Senator of the United States, whose last speech and vote were given, a few days before his death, against the territorial extension of slavery.

It was a good stock to spring from — for those grim religionists, who burned witches and Quakers, had in the old world smitten kings to preserve liberty, and in the new, laid the foundations of a democratic empire that now stretches over a continent. That imaginative temperament which peers into the unseen, and gives a mystical predominance to things of the spirit over things of the flesh, often blossoms into the loveliest flowers. Certainly to it we trace nearly all our foremost poets, from him

who, as a boy still, sung our first immortal song
amid the snow-drifts of the Hampshire hills, to
him, our Quaker Tyrtæus, who the other day
put off his singing-robes to take on a wreath of
unfading laurel.

Mr. Curtis's schooling outside of the home,
where he was a diligent reader of books, was
brief and scanty :* two years at a public academy, and one of private tuition ; but his edu-
cation was none the less wide-ranging, nutritious, and fruitful. As with nearly all men of
genius, it was a self-education and peculiar.
After a year's trial of a mercantile pursuit,
which proved repulsive, instead of going to college, he hurried, with a brother, to Brook Farm,
a small agricultural and educational association, recently gathered near Roxbury, Mass.† It

---

* He attended an academy at Jamaica Plains, near Boston,
for two years. His mother died while he was yet a child, and
the father married again, and in 1839 removed to New York
with his family. His father was cashier of one bank and afterwards president of another, and the lad could easily have gone
to college if he had wished.

† The immediate founders were the Rev. George Ripley
and his wife, Charles A. Dana, Wm. H. Channing, C. P.
Cranch, John S. Dwight, and others; but Theodore Parker,
Margaret Fuller, Bronson Alcott, Henry James the elder,
Albert Brisbane, Parke Godwin, etc., took a deep interest
in its success. All over the country, later, many citizens
attentively studied socialism, among whom I may mention
one who was afterwards distinguished as a soldier and states-

was an outcome of a socialistic wave rolling over Europe and America at the time, and, by its agitations, stirring up a good deal of foam, ooze, and amphibious drift-wood, with here and there a pearl of the sea like this. But it was nothing new on the face of the earth. In all ages generous minds, dissatisfied with the actual conditions of society, have endeavored to bring back a vanished golden age by a reconstruction of its methods; and the loftiest intellects have exerted their best faculties to discover the Aladdin's Lamp which could transform hovels into palaces. A man who has not, at some time of his youth, been convinced that he could lift society at once to a state of universal prosperity and happiness, has more of the clod in him than of the angel.

These New England reformers were tinctured by that mode of thinking which was called Transcendentalism, but which was not so much a creed as an emotional protest against the hard, metallic cast given to Calvinism by the severe Puritan intellect. But their practical arrangements were largely influenced by the speculations of Fourier, which had already

man and as the second of our martyr-Presidents, James A. Garfield.

formed a school in France, and were widely accepted in the United States.*

Hawthorne, in his "Blithedale Romance" —a fanciful story suggested by his own experiences at Brook Farm—calls its inmates "a knot of dreamers," and dreamers they were indeed, but of a beautiful dream. They hoped, by means of wiser and juster industrial and social arrangements, "to simplify economics, to combine leisure for study with healthful and honest toil, to avert unjust collisions of caste, equalize refinements, awaken generous affections, diffuse courtesy, and sweeten and sanctify life as a whole."† More disinterested aims never animated a body of cultivated men and women. The experiment proved to most of them merely a romantic episode in their lives, but one never to be forgotten. Mr. Curtis for nearly two years shared in their labors of the house and field, and in their instructions and studies; but was chiefly remembered by his companions for his sprightly leadership of picnics and masquerades, and his pleasant singing, after nightfall, of *romanzas* from the operas.

---

* Nearly fifty practical experiments under the impulse given by them were made, and failed in the end.

† Wm. H. Channing, in "Memoirs of Margaret Fuller."

He must have been benefited by the influences of that select and gentle circle, which appealed to the better tendencies of his naturally fine nature, and strengthened his interest in social questions; but while, in accordance with Schiller's noble advice, he always "reverenced the dreams of his youth," he never became a socialist. His experiences there convinced him, if we may judge by his after-conduct, that the best way to reform and elevate society, is not by withdrawing from it to a small coterie in a corner; but by breasting its tides as they come, and by laying one's heart against the great heart of humanity—to get from it the best inspirations it has to give, and to return to it the noblest ideals we can impart. Sects, parties, and conclaves which shut themselves off from the broad currents of life are apt to dwindle into narrowness and inanity, or, sooner or later, return to the broad bosom they had abandoned.

A second period in Mr. Curtis's plan of self-culture began when he left the happy family at Brook Farm — not yet dispersed by the frost-winds of a financial winter — to settle on a farm at Concord. His aim was partly to become a practical agriculturist, and partly to obtain more leisure and solitude for study. He might have procured a more classical tuition in the neighboring halls of Harvard; but he preferred that open university whose dome is the overarching blue, whose floors are the enamelled meadows, and whose chambers are the sylvan cloisters of the groves—shut in at eve by crimson curtains, and lit up all night by the silver lamps of heaven.

His text-books lay before him in the locality itself, teeming with nutritious patriotic memories. Every house of the small cluster of houses was inhabited by the descendants of those who landed "on the stern and rock-bound coast, when breaking waves dashed high"; the hills around had echoed the thunders of Adams and of Otis when they roused the colonists to arms; yonder highway was the road on which the hoofs of Paul Revere's horse clattered in his famous midnight ride; Lexington Green was but a few miles off, and daily before him stood the bridge where the "embattled farmers fired the shot heard round the world." It is to the study of this class-book I ascribe his rare familiarity with our Revolutionary annals, and his intense but high-toned Americanism — an Americanism which, not insensible to the grandeurs of Niagara, the Mississippi, the Rocky Mountains, and the sea-like lakes, where great ships sail out never to be heard of more, nor unmindful of that intelligence and brawny energy which converts the forests and the rocks into benignant human uses, yet finds its chief nutriment in those free democratic institutions which, emancipating the individual from the fetters of convention, give a larger scope than is to be found anywhere else to the development of the noblest manhood and womanhood.

He was particularly fortunate to find in this open-air college teachers not often to be met with in class-rooms — such as Emerson, the first philosopher of his time, who inwove with the insight and poetry of Plato an insight and poetry of his own, with a Rembrandt's power to paint, and ears that heard æolian harps in every whispering wind; as Hawthorne — our New England Prospero — who evolved out of the chill and desolate legends of Puritanism a whole new world of romance and fascination; as Thoreau, the woodland Diogenes — Plotinus-Orson, as Curtis called him — whose "quick ears and sharp eyes" had caught the deeper secrets of the forest; and as Margaret Fuller, among the most learned of women, who communed with Æschylus and Dante and Boccaccio and Beethoven, and aspired to ride in the flaming chariots of Goethe drawn by the coursers of the sun.

By two of these teachers our young scholar, just on the verge of manhood, must have been deeply impressed. Emerson had already put forth that thin little volume on " Nature," which bulges with suggestive thought as the branches in spring-time swell with the coming buds. A few of his strange poems had appeared, whose voices come down to us from the upper air, like the rough music of Pan when he pipes to the winds and the stars. He was even then engaged with those " Essays " * which have imparted so bracing, stimulating, and strengthening a tonic to the intellect of the century, and whose one great virtue, whatever their defects and inconsistencies, is to set men thinking with a desire to think aright.

Hawthorne was also at that time gathering his " Mosses from an Old Manse "—mosses that in his hands bloomed into the strangest orchidian shapes, and an old manse that rose

* The first series was published in 1841, the second in 1844.

on pillars of cloud—in many-gabled towers, through whose casements shone a moonlight haunted by witches and ghosts, grim, ghastly, and terrible, and yet with faces as beautiful as any which look from the pictures of Stuart and Copley. As Emerson had a power to incite thought; so Hawthorne had to incite imagination, but our impressible scholar, while he admired the serene and lofty tone of the one, and the weird and impassioned fantasy of the other, was inspired, not enslaved, by them; we find some traces of each in his writings, but only traces; and no one has written with more discrimination of them than he has since written. He wandered freely through their gardens of bloom; he inhaled with pleasure the perfume of their flowers, he sipped with ecstacy of " their lucent sirups, tinct with cinnamon," but he cherished his own ideals of truth and beauty, and turned away to find them by methods of his own. As he had not become a socialist at Brook Farm, so at the fountain-head of the sect he did not become a transcendentalist.*

---

* The reader will find in Hawthorne (" Old Manse "), Lowell (article on " Thoreau "), and Curtis (Emerson, in " Homes of American Authors ") most amusing accounts of the eccentrics that Emerson attracted to Concord—"Apostles of the Newness," and preachers of various kinds of bran-and-potato gospels.

Mr. Curtis's residence of four years in Europe and the East may be regarded as the third period of his self-culture. He sailed in 1846,* and was landed at Marseilles, whence he hastened to Italy, and then visited the greater part of western Europe, and of Egypt and Syria. Fruitful years they were indeed. As he travelled on foot when he could, or by diligence or market-boat, he saw much of the common people in their haunts and homes; he explored every quiet nook or sheltered valley or mountain-pass where beauty lingers, and every picturesque village or town or city which lives in history. Of course he loitered in the cathedrals where the twilight often breaks into organ peals or Gregorian chants, and the galleries where immortal genius had shattered the sunbeams upon canvas; he haunted the museums, the theatres, and the opera-houses; he attended courses of lectures at Leipsic and Berlin; and as one of his years was the famous revolutionary year of 1848, he saw at Paris the masses when they go down into the streets, and at Ber-

---

* He was accompanied by our late fellow-member—preacher, poet, artist, and musician—Mr. C. P. Cranch and his family, and in the East by his friend and, later, brother-in-law, Quincy Shaw. At Rome he fell in with Hicks and Kensett, also members of this club.

lin he heard the angry students sing by torch-
light

"A mighty fortress is our God,
    A trusty shield and weapon."

In 1850 he came back, laden like a foraging
bee with sweet burdens of language, art, literature, scenery, and society.

The flowers and fruits of this rich European
harvest have left their fragrance and savor in all
his subsequent work; but his Eastern gather-
ings he shared at once with the public, as a
sort of first-fruits of his apprentice and wander-
years. They were two remarkable volumes, pur-
porting to be books of travel,* and which, as
such, came into comparison with several reign-
ing favorites, such as the " Eothen " of King-
lake, " The Crescent and the Cross " of Eliot
Warburton, and the " Eastern Letters " of Har-
riet Martineau. But a comparison was hardly
possible, they were so different. Those books
were books of travel strictly, full of useful infor-
mation and the proper sentiments ; but these
books contained scarcely a description from
cover to cover. They furnished very little eru-

---

* " Nile Notes of a Howadji," 1851, and " The Howadji in
Syria," 1852.

dition as to Thothmes, Ramses, or the inter-
minable dynasties; they deciphered no hiero-
glyphics, unrolled no mummies, and penetrated
into no tombs ; but, plunging at once into the
voluptuous sunshine of the East, they shouted
with ancient Pistol,

> "A foutra for the world and worldlings base!
> I speak of Africa, and golden joys."

Their pages were all pictures and poetry—im-
pressionist pictures, a little hazy in form perhaps, but radiant with color—and poetry without rhyme, yet rhythmical as the song of birds
or the dance of waves on the strand. Whatever was peculiar in Eastern climate, landscape,
or life, you were made to feel with a vividness
it never had before ; and even generations mum-
mied ere our civilizations began masqueraded
like a new life in death.

Nor, in the tumult and rapture of sensuous im-
pressions, were the sacred traditions of place forgotten, and especially of Him who hovers over
human memory as the tranquil sweetness of a
summer sky hovers over the landscape. How
touching that passage which, after forty years,
recurs to me as I write, where, stretched by
night on the Syrian sands, the myriads of war-
like hordes that once trod them rise again—As-

syrians, Jews, Saracens, Persians, Arabs, Crusad-
ers, and Frenchmen—but, through "the flash
of cimeters, the cloud of hurtling arrows, and
the glittering Roman axes," the author sees
only, subduing emperors, kings, and sultans, the
figure of One who rode upon an ass, with no
sceptre but a palm-branch, and no crown but
a crown of thorns.

These first books gave Mr. Curtis position
and even fame as an author; but they sadly
puzzled some of the critics, who complained of
their excesses of color and sentiment—not seeing under the pomp of the garb the keen artistic sensitiveness, the opulent imagination,
and the subtle, swift-glancing fertility of thought
which rendered that pomp both necessary and
appropriate. But other critics felt with Keats,
on his first reading Chapman,

> ". . . like some lone watchers of the skies,
> When a new planet swims into their ken."

They were new in the extreme novelty of their
form and matter, and they were planetary in
their effulgence. That overfulness complained
of, like the buoyancy of youth, might be
chastened, but not exhausted, by maturity, and
promised a rich future. His next book, letters from the watering - places to a newspa-

per, and called "Lotus-Eating," glows with a similar, yet subdued, exuberance, deluging our landscape with "purpureal gleams," and seeing in the hotels the same men and women that he had seen when floating on the canals of Venice, stepping out of the canvases of Titian and Giorgione.

It was at this time (1851–52) that I became more intimately acquainted with Mr. Curtis, so that henceforth I shall be able to speak of him from personal reminiscences. It came about in this wise: An enterprising publisher of New York, Mr. Putnam, had projected a magazine of the highest class, which should take rank beside the *Blackwoods* and *Frasers* of the old world. We possessed some ponderous quarterlies like the *North American Review* and others, mainly organs of religious denominations, but the magazine proper had scarcely risen beyond the second story back of the milliner shops. It was a hazardous undertaking, but the publisher was brave and the scheme was carried into effect. Mr. Charles F. Briggs, better known as Harry Franco, from a forgotten novel of his, was asked to take the helm as manager, and Mr. Curtis and myself were given each a laboring oar. We gathered a goodly company of assistants around us, nearly all the known men of letters of the time,* and put forth a worthy pioneer of the more imposing ventures of to-day.

Mr. Curtis was at that time a great favorite in society—not of the fashionable sort he afterwards satirized, but of a higher grade, which had historical pretensions, and retained some of the old flowing colonial courtesy and culture. His fine figure, his handsome face, his polished address, his humorous talk, and growing fame as an author, got him easy access anywhere, or as Lowell has since rhymed it,

> "all the chariest doors
> Swung wide on flattered hinges to admit
> Such high-bred manners, such good-natured wit."

A few feared lest the adulations heaped upon

---

* It may interest those who are curious as to our literary history to add, that among our promised contributors—the most of whom complied with their promises—were Irving, Bryant, Emerson, Longfellow, Lowell, Hawthorne, Thoreau, George Ripley, Miss Sedgwick, Mrs. Kirkland, author of "A New Home: Who'll Follow?" J. P. Kennedy, author of "Swallow Barn"; Fred. S. Cozzens, of the "Sparrow-grass Papers"; Richard Grant White, "Shakespeare's Scholar"; Edmund Quincy, author of "Twice Married"; William Swinton, since the accomplished historian of "The Army of the Potomac"; Richard Kimball, Herman Melville, of "Typee" and "Omoo" fame, Richard Henry Stoddard, E. C. Stedman, Ellsworth, Thomas Buchanan Read, Maria Lowell, Jervis McEntee, and others. We had a strong backing from the clergy—the Rev. Drs. Hawks, Vinton, Hanson, Bethune, Baird, also the occasional assistance of Arthur Hugh Clough, the friend of

him should seduce him from the student's smoky lamp to Paphian bowers lit by gilded chandeliers and eyes more bright than jewels; but they knew little of his native good sense, his strong self-respect, and his broad sympathies, which would have saved him at any time from scorching his wings in any false glare, however flattering or seductive. He got out of society, as out of everything else, whatever he thought to be good, and the rest he let go to the ash-barrel.

I mention this to introduce a little incident that had a great deal to do in directing his future course. Our first number of the monthly had been a success; at least those arbiters, not merely of all elegancies, but of destiny itself—the daily press—had patted us on the back, and

---

Tom Hughes, Matthew Arnold, and other pupils of Dr. Arnold, who was then in this country—William Henry Herbert, reputed grandson of the Earl of Pembroke, sportsman and naturalist, known as Frank Forrester ; William North, a frank and brilliant young Englishman ; Fitz-James O'Brien, who died in our war for the Union, and Thomas Francis Meagher, a gallant soldier in the same war, and afterwards Governor of Montana. Miss Delia Bacon, whose unhappy history is told by Hawthorne in "Our Old Home," began her eccentric Shakespeare-Bacon controversy by a learned and brilliant article in the monthly. An article by Dr. Hanson, going to prove that the heir to the French throne, who was supposed to have been killed in the Tower, was still living as a St. Regis Indian (the Rev. Eleazer Williams), produced a great sensation both in the United States and France.

we set sail on halcyon seas and under favorable winds. It was while providing entertainment for our readers in a second number that the vivacious Harry Franco exclaimed, " I have it ! Let us, each of us, write an article on the state of parties. You, Howadji, who hang a little candle in the naughty world of fashion, will show it up in their light; you, Pathfinder, who consort with scurvy politicians, will say of it what they think ; while I will discuss it in some way of my own "—which he never did.

But Mr. Curtis and the other person were moved by the hint, and the former at once wrote a paper on the state of parties, which he called " Our Best Society." It was a severe criticism of the follies, foibles, and affectations of those circles which got their guests, as they did their edibles and carriages, from Brown, sexton and caterer, and which thought unlimited supplies of terrapin and champagne the test and summit of hospitality. Trenchant as it was, it was yet received with applause. Some thought the name of the leading lady more suggestive than facts warranted, and that in such phrases as " rampant vulgarity in Brussels lace," " the orgies of rotten Corinth," and " the frenzied festivals of Rome in her decadence," the brush was overloaded. None the less, the satire delighted the public, and was soon followed by other papers in the same vein—since collected as " The Potiphar Papers." The older folks acknowledged them to be the best things of the kind since Irving and his friends had taken the town with the whimwhams and conceits of Evergreen, Wizard, and the Cockloft family. They were to some extent exaggerations, in which occasional incidents were given as permanent features; but their high and earnest purpose, their genuine humor, their amusing details, their hits at characters, and their sarcasms, " deodorized of offensive personality " by constant drippings from the springs of fancy, won them great favor. If we behind the screen sometimes felt that we shook hands with the originals of Kurtz Pasha and the Reverend Cream-Cheese, they were, like sweet bully Bottom, marvellously translated.

All the while Mr. Curtis was flinging his squibs and crackers into Vanity Fair, he was wandering in a wholly different realm—a realm " of ampler ether and diviner air." He was writing for us, from time to time, papers of a much higher tone than any he had yet written, and which seemed to me, as I sometimes looked

over the proof-sheets, to open an entirely new
and rich vein in our literature. They were
those exquisite reveries since published under
the quaint title of "Prue and I." The main
conception, the *Leit-Motif*, as Wagner would
say, was as old as poetry and the arts—the
steeping of the palpable and familiar in the
glorious dyes of the ideal, which children's
fables, folk-lore, Middle-Age legends, and great
poets have done for us time out of mind; but
Mr. Curtis's treatment of his theme was quite
fresh and original and most captivating. His
shabby old book - keeper, in a faded cravat,
whose brain teems with visions

> "Of all that is most beauteous—imaged there
> In happier beauty,"

is one of the most delightful of dreamers. He
roams not in the fabled world of ancient poets,
peopled with oread or dryad fleet or naiad of
the stream, nor in the world of more modern
fancy, whose forest depths and fields and foun-
tains teem with fairy shapes of peerless grace
and cunning trickeries; but his caprices revel
in a sphere of their own, whence all rude neces-
sities are banished, and gentle passions and
sweet longings for the serene and joyous and
perfect reign alone. These are the Ariels

with which he rides on the winds and plays on the curled cloud. How quaint is that touch, worthy of Elia, where, going back to his boy-hood, he tells how he visited the wharves where the foreign ships come in, and returning home with a smell on his clothes, was chided by the good mother. He says : " I retired from the ma-ternal presence proud and happy. I was aro-matic. I had about me the true foreign air. Whoever smelt me smelt distant countries." With what a royal hospitality he sallied forth from his cold beef and cabbage to the avenues and squares where prosperous citizens were going to dinner, and furnished their tables more amply than those of any emperor. How the ladies in the gilded chariots, superb and sweet, each one his own Aurelia, seemed " fairer than the evening air, clad in the beauty of a thousand stars," while he lent to them a tongue like Perdita's, and the music of St. Cecilia her-self. Could anybody resist an invitation to his castles in Spain, which "stood lofty and fair in a luminous golden atmosphere, a little hazy and dreamy perhaps, like Indian summer, but where no gales blew and there were no tempests. All the sublime mountains and beautiful valleys and soft landscapes were to be found in the grounds. From the windows looked the sweet women whom poets have painted, and bands of celestial music played all night to enchant the brilliant company into silence." Mr. Franco and his colleague of the triumvirate used to look forward to these delightful papers, as one does to a romance " to be continued "; and when we received one of them, we chirruped over it, as if by some strange merit of our own we had entrapped a sunbeam. We followed the lines so intently, with such various exclamations of pleasure, that a stranger coming in might have suspected both of us to belong to that wonderful company of eccentrics which the old scrivener summoned from the misty realms of tradition—the Wandering Jew; the priests of Prester John; the alchemists who sought to turn base metals into gold; the hunters of El Dorado, of Enchanted Islands, of the Fountain of Perpetual Youth; the makers of Utopias ever looming up and ever vanishing; even our own Captain Symmes, who sails through his hole into the interior of the earth, where its jewels and precious metals are forged; and that famous friend of our childhood, the Baron Munchausen, whose signal claim to a place in a fictitious world was that he was the one most re-

plenished liar out of all the thousand millions
of humans—and brought them all together on
the deck of the *Flying Dutchman*, to sail forever through foggy seas, onward, onward to un-
known shores.*

It was an evidence of the fecundity and ver-
satility of Mr. Curtis's gifts, that while he was
thus carrying forward two distinct lines of in-
vention—the one full of broad comic effects,
and the other of exquisite ideals—he was con-
tributing to the entertainment of our public in
a half-dozen other different modes — monthly
criticisms of music and the drama that broadened the scope and raised the tone of that form
of writing; rippling Venetian songs that had
the swing of the gondola in them; crispy short
stories of humor or pathos; reminiscences of
the Alps taken from his Swiss diaries; elaborate reviews of books, like Dickens's " Bleak
House," the Brontë novels, Dr. Veron's Mé-
moires, Hiawatha, and recent English poetry—
including that of Kingsley, Matthew Arnold,
Thackeray, the Brownings, and Tennyson —

---

* There is something similar to this in Hawthorne's "A
Select Party," where Funnyman asks the Oldest Inhabitant,
Monsieur On Dit—the Clerk of the Weather, Davy Jones, the
Man of Straw, and others to a banquet in his palace—which
is more diverting perhaps, but less imaginatively pathetic.

which, written forty years ago, have not been surpassed since by more appreciative, discriminating, and sympathetic criticism, even in that masterly and more elaborate book of our fellow-member, "The Victorian Poets." In addition to these, he gave us, from time to time, solid and thoughtful discussions of "Men of Character," of "Manners," of "Fashion," of the "Minuet and the Polka" as social tide-marks, and of "Rachel," which may still be read with instruction and pleasure for their keen observation, their nice critical discernment, their cheerful philosophy, and their entrancing charms of style.

Then, ever and anon, Mr. Curtis would be off for a week or two, delivering lectures on "Sir Philip Sidney," on "The Genius of Dickens," on "The Position of Women," and, in one case, a course of lectures in Boston and in New York on "Contemporary Fiction." In a galaxy of lecturers which included Emerson, Phillips, Beecher, Chapin, Henry Giles, and others, he was a bright particular star, and everywhere a favorite. A harder-working literary man I never knew; he was incessantly busy; a constant, careful, and wide reader; yet never missing a great meeting or a great address or a grand night at the theatre. From our little

4

conclaves at No. 10 Park Place, where I fear we remorselessly slaughtered the hopes of many a bright spirit (chiefly female), he was seldom absent, and when he came he took his full share of the routine—unless Irving, Bryant, Lowell, Thackeray, or Longfellow sauntered in, and "that day we worked no more."

We now approach a wholly different phase of our friend's activity—less agreeable than the others, but more important, and a phase which shows how brave, manly, and noble he could be in the face of the most alluring literary and social seductions. Up to the time of his joining us in *Putnam* he had taken no part in politics. Like his friends Lowell and Longfellow, who had written, the one " Biglow Papers," with a fervor that almost raised slang into a classic, and the other " Hymns of Slavery," which brought tears to the eyes—though tears have never yet rusted away the chains of the captive—he was intensely anti-slavery in feeling. But his opinions had not yet crystallized into definite shape. So far as he had any politics at all, they were a general acquiescence with the Whig school as interpreted by Seward, who was still a watcher of times and seasons. Like all scholars, he felt what Milton has described as " an unwillingness to leave the quiet and still air of delightful studies to embark on a troubled sea of noises and harsh disputes." Yet he was one of those who. thought that a man of letters had something else to do in this world than to sing love-ditties to Amaryllis in the shade, or paint pretty pictures for the cultured classes.

Be that as it may, it was impossible for a man of genius and soul, at that day, to resist the great ground-swell of popular passion fast coming to the surface. Those years, from 1848 to 1860, were years of revival and resuscitation, when the American people went back to breathe the invigorating air of their early days. Let me recall—at least for those too young to remember—how tangled and terrible our political condition was, and how it had been brought about.

Our fathers had deliberately founded this nation on the great central, pervasive, and distinguishing idea of right as transcending interest, and of equal popular rights as the origin, the basis, and the aim of all good government; yet they had allowed the nation to carry in its flanks a monstrous evil, in flat and disgraceful contradiction of its fundamental principles. Their excuse was the belief that free institutions would inevitably work out its speedy extinction. But that hope was a delusion. Slavery, instead of yielding to the influences of freedom, struck its roots deeper into the soil, and began to stretch forth its dead-man's fingers to the heart-strings of the people. Claiming a constitutional guarantee, interwoven with vast commercial interests, fortified by inveterate prejudices of race, it grew so rapidly in power that it soon assumed to control conventions, dictate policies, elect congressmen and presidents, and prescribe opinion. The South was riding the nation as the Old Man of the Sea rode on the shoulders of Sindbad.

Then came those days, "never to be recalled without a blush," when the politicians bowed down to it as to an idol, and worshipped it; when the counting-houses fawned upon it, that thrift might follow fawning; when the Press decorated its hideous brows with wreaths of praise, and even the Pulpit wove around it the sanctions of Holy Writ. The panting fugitive, guided by the North Star, fled from bloodhounds and deadly morasses, and came to our homes to beg for refuge; we were told to return him to bondage—and we did it. Our virgin territories —the homes of a vast future civilization—

whose soil was yet unwet by the blood of the bondman, and its dews unstained by his tears, were claimed as the rightful abodes of the curse—and we acquiesced.

Of course these atrocities provoked reaction. Side by side with the black stain in our history ran a line of white which brightened and broadened each day. Individuals protested, even when they were killed for it; small sects remembered that Christianity was a gospel of brotherhood, not of hatred; the Abolitionists made their frantic appeals to the moral sense; Liberty-men resorted to the ballot-box; Conscience-Whigs undermined the old Whig Party as Free-soil Democrats were undermining the old Democratic Party; but as yet they were all working apart and at loose ends. Traditional prejudices and mutual misunderstandings kept them asunder. Many of them even hoped that the dispute could be compromised and the conflict adjourned.

Our little world of the Monthly was profoundly stirred by these agitations of the outer world. For the first time in the history of our higher periodicals, its managers had stepped down from their snowy pedestals to take part in the brabble and scuffle of the streets; and it raised an almost universal outburst of vituperation and censure. As Lamb said of his play, "Great heavens, how they did hiss!" For a time it seemed as if the little bark was destined to go down amid the roaring and foaming rocks.*

The offence and the service of the Monthly, speaking the sentiments of large and increasing classes of literary and professional people, was, that while the old parties shilly-shallied, it had steadfastly and stubbornly insisted that no conciliation between the free and the slave States was possible or desirable. The conflict was an irrepressible conflict. Our political system, in bringing together under the same rule two incompatible forms of civilization, had yoked Pegasus, the winged horse of the gods, to a drudge ox, and they would not and could not pull together. There was but one thing

---

* It happened while Mr. Curtis had been ministering to the delight of our readers in many ways and receiving showers of applause in return, that another one of the triumvirate, taken by Mr. Franco's suggestion, had written his version of the state of parties, and called it "Our New President." It was a criticism of Mr. Pierce, who had recently been elected, not for Democratic depravity in general, but for the reckless license he had shown in distributing the sacred trusts of office to a parcel of heelers and hoodlums, whose only desert was that they had voted the regular ticket, and stood ready to mangle and maul any one who did not join with them in

to do, in the actual condition of things, and that was for the friends of freedom, of every name and description, to sink their party differences, to unite in a new party—to nail the glorious device of " Free soil, free speech, free men" to their banners, and march to victory. " But oh !" cried the timider souls, "that means civil war!" "And if it does," was the reply, " never strike sail to a fear! Come into port grandly, or sail with God the seas."

Events soon brought about the consummation so devoutly wished. Free-minded Whigs and free-minded Democrats and others joined hands in 1854–55, to form the new Republican Party, and in 1856 designated the young Pathfinder of the West, who had nailed the flag of freedom on the highest peaks of the Rocky Mountains, to carry it in triumph to the Capitol. That auspicious union filled older, perhaps wiser, certainly more conservative,

---

that ceremony. This article raised a fierce outcry of opposition; but the commander, though he had values on board, was a brave soul, and said, " Brace up, my lads! Put her head one point nearer to the wind and crowd on sail!"— which we did accordingly—but without appeasing the northwesters. A succession of papers on " Parties and Politics," perhaps more verjuicy than juicy; on "Our American Despotism," meaning slavery; on " Kansas—It Must be Free "; and "The Two Forms of Society, Which ?" only aggravated the original scream of protest into a fierce howl of rage.

minds with horror and dismay; they heard only "ancestral voices prophesying woe," and saw Spectres of the Brocken, that seemed to rise like demons from the pit. But to younger, perhaps more visionary, minds it seemed, to use De Quincey's phrases, "as if the morning had come of a mighty day full of awakening suspense and busy preparation, a day of crisis and of final hope," when infinite cavalcades went filing off and they heard the march of innumerable armies, and in the distance a din of "battle, and agony, and sudden death," followed by a grand burst of coronation hymns signalizing victory.

Mr. Curtis's great opportunity had now come, and it came almost without his knowing it. He had fully approved the wild dashes of the Monthly against the Gibraltar rocks of the old parties, but he had written nothing as yet; and while he was in the habit of reading beautiful lectures from the written page, he distrusted his ability to speak from the platform. By the merest accident, at a Republican meeting on Staten Island, he was suddenly and vociferously called upon for an address. He ascended the steps with trembling; he stammered a few commonplaces for a while, "his practised accents throttled by his fears," and then his good genius came to his aid, and he poured forth an invective against slavery which filled his hearers with an unquenchable fire.* From that hour his course was clear, and he entered into the Fremont campaign with an inexpressible fearlessness and ardor; he spoke from stump to stump; he spoke by night and by day, and he spoke with a force of eloquence that he has never since equalled. But oh, what a battle it was! You have had a presidential campaign recently, which was milk and honey compared to that of fire and hail, in which a vast social system, the continuance of the government, the integrity of the nation itself, were at stake.

---

* His first discourse after that was at the Wesleyan University (Middletown, N. Y., Aug., 1856), where he had been invited to speak on "The Duties of the American Scholar." "Gladly would I speak to you," he said, "of the charms of scholarship, of the dignity and worth of the scholar—of the abstract relation of the scholar to the State. . . . But would you have counted him a friend of Greece who quietly discussed the abstract nature of patriotism on that summer day through whose hopeless and immortal hours Leonidas and his three hundred stood at Thermopylæ for liberty? . . . Freedom has always its Thermopylæ, and the American scholar should know that the American Thermopylæ is Kansas." That clarion voice echoed through all the colleges and among the hills, and had a great effect in arousing young men to the greatness of the existing contest.

Fortunately we failed in that attempt—fortunately, because the nation was not quite ready yet, and Fremont was not an adequate leader. But it prepared the way for the Lincoln campaign in 1860, which was scarcely less strenuous and violent. Mr. Curtis had shown his power on the stump; he now showed it in the convention, when at Chicago he put pandemonium to defeat, and bid the wild uproar be ruled.

All through the inevitable war he did what he could to urge on its vigorous prosecution. Nor was this service at a distance from the seat of war a perfunctory service. It had its sorrows and its sufferings. From his own family a cherished brother, Joseph Curtis, in the prime of youth; from the noble family into which he had married, no less dear to him,* three of its inmates in life's dawn of hope and promise—Shaw, Lowell, and Barlow—had gone to the front; and from his immediate circle others, like the brilliant Theodore Winthrop, dripping with genius, were gripping their sabres on the outposts. Any day's bulletins might bring—some days'

---

*In 1857 Mr. Curtis was married to Annie, a daughter of Francis G. Shaw, of Staten Island.

bulletins did bring — irreparable heartaches. Four of the five young heroes fell in the fierce joy of battle, to pass to an immortal youth. But through all vicissitude and anguish his voice still helped to ram the cannon home, to cheer the poor brother in the trenches, to push forward the shining tents of light into the frowning darkness.

It seems as if such excitements must have distracted him from literary pursuits, but these had now become only the more regular and exacting. Since 1853, Mr. Curtis, without severing his connection with *Putnam*, had written in a desultory way for *Harper's Magazine*, and he finally accepted an editorial department of it, called the Editor's Easy Chair. It was the name given to a form of literary work which, begun by a Frenchman, Montaigne, who is still first in merit as he was first in time, has long been a favorite with English readers: the short essay on minor topics of social interest which takes up offences too light for the censorship of the pulpit and too harmless for the chastisements of the law. It is a form which Addison, Steele, Johnson, Goldsmith, Lamb, Irving, and Thackeray have made exceedingly attractive. The eighty or hundred volumes of the British Essayists which have stood the sand-blasts of time lie side by side, in every respectable library, with the eighty or hundred volumes of the British poets. Carlyle has somewhere compared the editor to the vagrant preacher who sets up his booth in any field, and utters his wisdom or unwisdom to all who choose to hear. But the editor of the Easy Chair preached no sermons, or nothing that had in it the stiffness and super-sanctity of the sermon. It was rather the flowing and genial talk of the well-informed scholar, who was also the well-bred gentleman, turned critic and commentator. It was talk in many styles, critical, historical, humorous, grave, fanciful; in short, in every style except that which Voltaire declares the only bad one—the wearisome. Our friend was never dull, but always elastic, cheerful, enlivening; with fewer ways of being tedious, and more of being entertaining, than any of his predecessors. He had, it seems to me, all the elegance of Addison with less of his coldness and a heartier glow; all the sprightliness of Steele, with a richer humor and a keener sense of moral values; but to find his proper parallels we must come down to Goldsmith, Lamb, Irving, and Thackeray. How many thousands gladly recall what a privilege and delight it has been for many years to have this commentator visit them every month, to tell them what to admire and what to impugn, and to inspire them as they sat in their own easy-chairs with kindlier feelings towards their fellows, to dissipate the blues of business or public affairs, and to send them to bed with buoyant hopes for the morrow! What pleasant companionship he helped us to form with the forgotten poets, from whom he would furnish little-known but delicious verses; with misprized story-tellers like that fine fellow, Fielding, despite his bedraggled clothes; or with our childhood's friend, dear old John Bunyan! How we would visit with him at the Brownings in Florence, or get a chatty letter from them, or go out to supper with that grim old ogre and cynic, Titmarsh, and find him to be, after all, one of the most simple and kindly of men; or hear the famous Boz read once more of Pickwick and Sam and Buzfuz and the widder! How he made the stately Everett come before us and speak over again one of his pieces, with all the attitudes and gestures rightly put in; or the fiery Phillips wield his keen, incisive, glittering rapier—but bloodless now! As for the mimic world of the stage, so entrancing to many of us,

he would ring his little bell, and the curtain would
rise, and the elder Booth or the elder Wallack
would reappear, for this time only; or the younger Booth, with his matchless elocution, recite a
bit of Hamlet; or Mrs. Kemble give to Shakespeare a new delight by her recitations; or the
dear old John Gilbert revive Sir Peter or Sir
Anthony till your sides ached; or Jefferson
sidled on as poor Rip, to make the heart as well
as the sides ache. Now and then he would take
you aside and whisper slyly into your ear the
gossip of the sylphs of the season at Newport,
or turn the key into enchanted chambers where
the echoes still lingered of voices long silent—of
Pasta and Grisi and Sontag and Jenny Lind,
and where Thalberg and Sivori and Ole Bull
once played—in short, open a thousand sources
of keen and noble enjoyment.

You may say, perhaps, that any editor of a
periodical can play this showman's part. Oh,
yes; but not with the inexhaustible variety of
matter, the inimitable grace of manner, of Curtis.
His superiority was shown when, called away
altogether, the whole literary world asked, "And
who can take his place?" and the whole literary world answered, "No one." Well might
that world feel kindly towards him, for in all

those forty years he had made and left no rank-
ling wound.   If any one was to be reproved, he
was reproved with a smile that took away the
sting.   Even

> "The stroke of death was like a lover's pinch,
> Which hurts and is desired."

When a cancer was to be cut out, it was cut
out with the surgeon's delicate lancet, and never
with the soldier's sword, much less with the
butcher's cleaver.   In fact, he taught us how to
censure, and censure severely, but without bit-
terness, as he taught us how to jest without a
grimace, and to instruct without pedantry or
assumption.

It was observed of the Easy Chair that no
allusion was ever made by it to passing politics,
even when

> "The day was filled with slaughter,
> And the night-sky red with flames,"

excepting, perhaps, by a picturesque glance at
departing troops, or a shadow of disaster moving over the page like an ominous cloud.   The
pleasant, graceful talk went rippling on its way,
as fresh as a mountain brook through daisied
meadows; and you might have supposed the
genial talker cosily seated in some rustic retreat

amid cooling dews and odorous grasses, and
listening to the songs of birds and the musical
whispers of the winds. But all the while he
was in the centre of strife.

Towards the close of the war (1863) he had
accepted the exclusive political control of *Harper's Weekly*, and was thus brought in direct
contact with public affairs. It was a stirring
time, but a most trying time for statesmen and
publicists. The war itself had been a spectacle
of terrible grandeur; there were in the valor
and self-sacrifice of the troops, and the calm
confidence of the people in their cause, features
of moral sublimity; and the magnificent result
of the war—the emancipation of a continent
justified its awful cost, and made us proud of a
nation capable of such sacrifices in defence of
a noble and heroic idea. But after the war,
from the martyrdom of Lincoln to that of Garfield, came a period of almost universal disloca-
tion—at the South, of all the usual machinery
of civic and social life; and at the North, of all
the usual political opinions. Questions arose
as to how we should weld the broken pieces
again—questions of formidable magnitude and
extreme difficulty. There a horde of freedmen,
ignorant, illiterate, and who had never taken care

of themselves, was endowed with the franchise, to become the prey of carpet-bag adventurers, to whom the ballot-box was but another name for the dice-box; here a whole new generation, who had never seen a gold coin, was asked to decide as to the disposition of an enormous debt and a deluge of paper money. For the first time in our history, a president was impeached and tried for swinging round the circle, as he called a whirligig of vagaries; for the first time in our history, a great historical party became so lost to self-respect, to consistency of principle, to sanity of mind, that it made its standard-bearer of a life-long and inveterate enemy, with whom it had no sentiment in common; and, for the first time in our history, the presidency itself was made, through fraud and violence, a foot-ball of factions which brought the ship of state again into the troughs of the sea, and summoned the clouds with their lightnings to the horizon.

In this uncertain and perilous condition of affairs it was almost a providential benefaction that a journal having thousands of exchanges and nearly half a million weekly readers should have been put in the hands of a person so clear-sighted, so well-balanced, so honest, and so courageous as Mr. Curtis. With many of his conclusions at the time I did not agree. He was of the old Federalistic school, which put its confidence more in the mere forms of law than in the saving instincts and good sense of the people, and his distrust of the Democratic party, largely justified by recent events, amounted to prejudice; but I was glad, even while sometimes fighting him in the press, to recognize his high-mindedness, his impartiality, his conscientious adherence to his convictions, and his knightly courtesy and manly frankness. His influence was great, because his readers felt that every word he said was the truth as he understood it. His editorial articles were models of political discussion, always calm, serious, and earnest, with nothing of the hurried superficiality, the disingenuous perversions that often mark the newspaper style. They met every question face to face without disguising its difficulties or giving a partisan turn to any of its aspects. They taunted no one; they sneered at no one; they argued openly, fairly, generously with all. Their author seemed, indeed, to have but one ambition, which was to lift our politics to the highest level of dignity and honor.

As soon as Mr. Curtis was satisfied that the

proper fruits of the war would be gathered and
garnered, and

"The sacred pillars of the commonwealth
Stand readjusted on their ancient poise,"

his attention was turned to certain administra-
tive reforms which seemed to require instant
action. A chief, almost exclusive, object of his
solicitude was the condition of the civil service,
which was deplorable to the last degree. Methods of distributing public office had come into
vogue utterly at war with any true theory of popular institutions, with any right constitution of
political parties, and with the uniform practice
of the Fathers of the Republic. They were the
application to practical politics of the maxims of
ancient and barbaric warfare, which proclaimed
that to the victor belonged the spoils of the
enemy. Forty years ago, in writing of the subject, the present speaker asked: " Need any one
attempt to describe the disastrous effect of such
a practice on all the functions of public life?
Does it not attack political virtue at its source;
corrupt the integrity of the political body; in-
flame controversies which should be the debate
of great principles into intemperate and violent
personal hatreds; convert popular suffrage into
a farce, or, what is worse, into a falsehood and

a fraud; introduce the most unworthy agents into the most responsible trusts; bring a scandal upon government, and thereby weaken, if it does not wholly destroy, the sanctity of law?" This argument was illustrated by a reference to the metropolis, where " a nest of profligates and gamesters had baffled juries, baffled courts, baffled legislatures, and contemned public opinion in their shameless career of peculation."

Of course such results were deprecated by many of our more eminent statesmen, and as far back as 1835 Mr. Calhoun, in his famous report on " Executive Patronage," denounced the methods in which they originated with the utmost lucidity and vehemence. " Were a premium offered," he said, " for the best means of subverting liberty and establishing despotism, no scheme more perfect could be devised." In this view he was joined by Webster, Clay, and other eminent statesmen of all parties. In fact, the best traditions of all parties were against the practice.

But the most pernicious tendency of the system they did not foresee, and that was the aggrandizement of the king-maker rather than of the king; or, in other words, the evolution of that most anomalous of all political creatures, the party boss. It brought into existence an order of men who, without having performed any public services—who were neither soldiers, statesmen, great merchants, nor captains of industry — who, without possessing any signal ability or virtue, except the ability to conspire and to intrigue, and the virtue of a shameless impudence, are able, by the promise of spoils, to combine their corps of janissaries in such a way as to empower them to dictate terms to assemblymen, congressmen, judges — nay, to presidents, the august embodiments of the majesty and the might of the people.

Mr. Curtis was an earnest observer of this last development, and he had no need to go abroad for proofs of its iniquity. Object-lessons—a sort of kindergarten of deviltry—were hourly before him. He lived through the career of one Tweed, a coarse, vulgar, ignorant, and reckless adventurer, who, scarcely able to make a living by an honest mechanical trade, had yet, by the use of a party organization and the doctrine of spoils, made himself the political dictator of the city and, to a considerable extent, of the State. He designated aldermen, assemblymen, judges, and all the lesser occupants of bureaus, i. e., he determined who should make, interpret, and execute the laws, turning all the great functions of government into a means of enriching himself and his fellow-conspirators. This Panama scandal, which is to-day shaking France to the core, had its prototype in our city court-house, whose every stone was laid in a mortar of corruption, and every nail driven by purchased and infamous hands. So complete was the ascendency of one man that, when the better members of his party protested against his outrages, he replied with a sardonic leer, " And what are you going to do about it?"

It is true that Tweed and his harpies were ultimately dislodged, his legislators deposed and dogged by the curses of after-time, his judges impeached, his immediate friends imprisoned or exiled; but not until they were well gorged, and after years of effort on the part of one of our most astute and persistent statesmen. Even then, while the particular brood was killed, the cockatrice's egg remained uncrushed. Tweed had, and still has, his imitators in every State, city, and town in the nation, and their iron grip is fastened almost as firmly as ever upon parties—but not quite, thank Heaven and the untiring zeal of the Civil-Service reformers!

It was in vain to ask Congress or other legislative bodies to abolish the nuisance, because so many of their members were made by the machine, and no one likes to kill his creator. Even when it was not so, the interest in the reform was abstract, indirect, impersonal, and a matter of general principle confined to a few, while the interest in the evil itself was immediate, personal, profitable, and shared by many. It took forty years of strenuous struggle before Mr. Thomas Allen Jencks, of Rhode Island, could secure the appointment of a Civil-Service Commission to inquire into the nature of the abuses under federal rule, and to suggest remedies. Mr. Curtis was at once indicated as a member of that commission, and, appointed to it by President Grant, was chosen its chairman. We have seen the determination and energy he applied to the uprooting of slavery; and here was another form of it—not so patent or repulsive, far more subtle, and scarcely less destructive of the moral fibre of the nation—to which he gave the same fearlessness and fervor of antagonism. His first report, in 1871, as an exposition of the evil, and of the proper mode of correcting it, was a sort of *magna charta* of reform. Its logic was never answered, and could not be; indeed, its argument of the constitutional points involved was in substance, and almost in terms, adopted by the Court of Appeals in this State, and afterwards by the Supreme Court of the United States. But of what avail? General Grant was sincere in his approval of the change, but he found that his interference had stirred up a nest of hornets more formidable than the bullets of his fifty battles. His call for appropriations to carry on the struggle was flung in his teeth by Congress, his zeal abated, and Mr. Curtis was compelled to resign.

His zeal, however, did not abate. Too much had been done towards the introduction of the reform into the federal bureaus to warrant an abandonment of it; and for ten years, as president of the national league and of the local league, his efforts were incessant and effective. His annual addresses, in the former capacity, were models of appeal—crammed with pertinent facts, with impregnable proofs, with withering sarcasms, with irresistible eloquence. They so held all executive officers up to the line of duty that many of them, ashamed to do openly what party exigences required, resorted to shifts and subterfuges to hide their cowardice.

In assuming this position of censorship, Mr. Curtis came in conflict with the party of his predilection, and saw no alternative but to break away from it altogether; that, however, was no easy step. He admitted the necessity of parties; but he held, too, that the basis of party itself must be reason and conscience. Allegiance to party, carried beyond that point, became infidelity to one's own soul, and treason to the best interests of the nation. Willingly had he given to his party the careful study, the patient toil, the persuasive eloquence, the burning enthusiasm of his best days; but one thing he would not sacrifice to any party —his sense of right and wrong as a moralist, his independence as a citizen, his self-respect as a man. Denounce him you might, ridicule him, ostracise him, fill his post-bag with the garbage of the gutter, and yet would he trust in that interior monitor which is the highest rule of duty we can know or even conceive. But for men of this high tone, whom the poor sticklers for use and wont are apt to decry,

> "The dust of antique time would lie unswept,
> And mountainous Error be too highly heaped
> For truth to overpower."

Mr. Curtis's disappointment with the action

7

of Republican leaders as to the civil service led his mind to serious distrust of the policy of the Republican party on other questions, which, as they are still pending, we cannot discuss at this time. Suffice it to say that he was compelled, in 1884, to announce that he could not support its candidate for the Presidency, and in 1888, that he must support the candidate of the opposition. But in thus taking an attitude of complete superiority to all parties, he thenceforth stood before the public as the champion of Independence, to which he kept

"constant as the northern star . . .
That unassailable holds in his rank
Unshaked of motion."

Indeed, his mind seemed to open more and more fully as he advanced to that most vital and salutary of all social truths—that while organizations are indispensable to the attainment of certain great human ends, the individual person is always higher than any organization— and for the simple reason that the man is the End, and the organization only the Means. Therefore it is, that when you put the means above the end, you reverse the true order of life, you raise power above right, and open and ease the way to innumerable and destructive tyrannies. The grandeur of his position, de- nounced by partisans, was, after his death, rec- ognized by the newspapers of nearly every fac- tion when they spoke of him—as Lowell had previously spoken of him in verse — as "the Great Citizen." He was the great citizen be- cause he had dared to be the honest citizen, and a nobler epitaph " nor marble nor brass nor parchment " ever bore.

Mr. Curtis owed his successes to the voice no less than to the pen, and this address would be exceedingly imperfect if it did not dwell for a moment on his peculiar oratory. " Eloquence," he somewhere says, "is the supreme charm of speech," giving it precedence over song, " but where the charm lies is the most delusive of secrets. It is the spell of the magician, but it is not in his wand or in his words. It is the tone of the picture, it is the rhythm of the poem. It is neither a statement nor an argument, nor a rhetorical, picturesque, or passionate appeal. It is all these penetrated and glowing with the power of living speech—a magnetism, a fasci- nation, a nameless delight."

But however it is to be explained, I can bear witness to the fact in his case. It has been my good fortune to hear many of the foremost speakers of the age—from Kossuth, the prince of all, to Gladstone, Bright, Thiers, Channing, Everett, Webster, Choate, Sumner, Beecher, Phillips, Seargent Prentiss, and last, though not least, Robert Ingersoll; and while I recognize in several of them certain qualities which Mr. Curtis did not attain—in some a majesty and massiveness of movement like that of a great ship-of-war bearing gallantly down into the battle, in others the impetuous energy which, like a deep and swollen river, sweeps all before it, and in others again an intensity of pathos which renders every sentence tremulous with tears—it may be said of Mr. Curtis, with-out extravagance of praise, that for a certain sustained elevation and dignity, for uniformity of grace and unruffled fulness and richness of charm, he had few peers. His greatest effort, as I recall it now, was the eulogy he delivered on your late venerable president, Mr. Bryant, at the Academy of Music. A more brilliant or distinguished assemblage was never gathered in that once famous temple of art—comprising the rival claimants for the presidency, governors, judges, and the picked representatives of the professional, literary, and artistic classes, and circling zones of whatever was beautiful in our female world. His subject was not one of those that are usually thought necessary to arouse the best energies of a speaker—no invasion of Philip, no conspiracy against the mistress of the world, no cruel tyrant hanging like a cloud on the declivities of the hills, no separation of mother country and daughter colonies, no calling of a nation to arms—only the character of a simple citizen whose victories were those of the pen. Yet for an hour and a half that vast and diversified audience was held in rapt attention; not a silvery word or a golden image was lost; and when he closed with an impressive passage there was a solemn hush as if all were expectant of more, a pause that called to mind Milton's oft-quoted description of the effect of Raphael's discourse on our first parent, when he left his voice so charming in Adam's ear that for a while he

"Thought him still speaking, still stood fixed to hear."

It was a suspense of nature preceding a thunder-break of applause.

Under the immediate influence of the spell, one was ever too full of the pleasure to undertake to analyze, or even to wish to analyze, its sources, and only in cooler moments, when the effect had passed off, could he recall them. He would then, perhaps, remember the liquid and equable flow of the voice, pure and rich in tone, distinct in enunciation, and melodious in inflection and cadence; the limpid simplicity and purity of the language, at the same time sinewy and strong; the kindled eye and the rapid changes of feature answering to each emotion as it arose; the play and flash of imagery, like lightning in a summer cloud—never brought in as mere ornament, but arising spontaneously as the only possible vehicle of the thought; the thought itself, always natural, apposite, and impressive, but borne on some wave of feeling which pulsated through each sentence like rich blood in the cheeks of a sensitive woman; the felicity of the allusions or quotations, each one of which was like turning on a new shade of color; and then the perfect symmetry and completeness of the whole—no part obtrusive, no part deficient—and all presented with such an absence of apparent effort, such consummate ease and grace of delivery, that no room was left in the mind of the hearer for any emotion but that of admiration and delight.

Complimenting him, after the delivery of

his eulogy on Bryant, on the perfectness of the performance, he modestly replied, " Dear friend, it was the occasion of my life "—which was doubtless true as to circumstances; but the phrase conveyed to me the open secret of his life. He was so supremely, thoroughly, and unconsciously the artist, that every occasion was an occasion, if not the occasion, of his life. By the mere instinct of artistic fitness he made his preparations so carefully and completely; his respect for his audience, however composed, was so profound, his fidelity to his own ideals so exacting, that he was ever at his best. He could no more have offered an uncombed or slovenly speech than he could have come forward uncombed and slovenly in person; or than a great painter could hang a daub on the walls of an exhibition, or a true poet put forth a poem with rheumatism in its feet. I have no doubt that those who afterwards heard his eulogies of Sumner, Phillips, and Lowell, or his oration at the Washington Monument or on the Saratoga battle-field, or his several addresses to the Civil Service League, thought as I did at the Bryant Commemoration—that they had got him in his happiest mood. Even on lesser occasions—a dinner of the Chamber of Commerce, of the Academy of Design, or of a college fraternity—he was sure to be up to expectation, if he did not surpass it; and when he mingled some touches of humor, some quips and quirks of merriment, in his discourse, they were certain to be set in an enchased framework of gold and silver. How often at a simple symposium of a few good fellows, when George, as we familiarly called him, was talking, it seemed as if we sat under a gorgeous summer sky, with murmurs of music in all the air.

Mr. Curtis was most happily endowed for the production of effects upon others, either as a writer or a speaker. His mind was both acute and vigorous, but it was planted in a soil richly sensitive, imaginative, and emotional. His turn of thought was not philosophical, i. e., metaphysical or speculative; he never dug down to what Schopenhauer called " the fourfold roots of the sufficient reason," and the very phrase would have amused him; but none the less he had a philosophy of his own—that natural-idealism or ideal-naturalism which is the philosophy of all artists who see consciousness in nature and nature in consciousness; and for whom the smile, which is a pure delight of the mind, exists also in the sparkle of the eye and the curve of the lips. His intellectual life came to him from no mysterious pineal gland hidden away in the folds of the brain, but from the tremulous fibres of the senses, whose manifold, many-colored, many-toned messages were taken up by that imperial wizard and artificer, the fantasy — and, by some secret alchemy, dissolved and wrought over again into manifold, many-colored, many-toned words.

It is not to be inferred from this that Mr. Curtis's reasoning powers were inferior; he seized readily upon general principles, but not the profoundest nor the most abstract, only the middle sort, the *axiomata media*, which connect the more obvious aspects of things and lie open to common-sense. He could argue well, as many an adversary found to his cost, but not at long breath ; he preferred figures of rhetoric to figures of logic, and drew men by the lyre of Apollo rather than drove them by the club of Hercules. They were the more easily drawn because, through all the glow and glamour of his sensuous and imaginative showings there pierced such a solid aspiration for what is permanently commanding in nature and permanently ennobling in conduct, and such a fixed, instinctive, unaffected love of truth, that he commanded at the same time that he won adherence and homage.*

The career I have roughly outlined—though full, well-rounded, and beautiful—gives but an imperfect image of the man as he was in himself, in his humble home, and in his private intercourse with friends. Nothing he ever wrote or spoke or did was so dear to those who knew him intimately as "the soft memory of his virtues," in which so many varied elements kindly mingled. Simple and guileless as a child, sweet, modest, and lovable as a woman, loyal and devoted to his friends, generous and without guile to his enemies, and uniformly courteous to all, he carried with him everywhere an atmosphere of cheerfulness that was as invigorating as a mountain breeze. Punctual in the discharge of the lowliest as of the highest duties, working for thirteen years

---

* If we were disposed to criticise his intellectual constitution, one might say that he was, particularly in early life, overcharged with sentiment that came near to sentimentality. His personal emotions were then so strong that he was not able to master them completely or to be dramatic. His novel, called "Trumps," was a proof of this: although written with extreme grace, and abounding in exquisite scenes and descriptions, it was not a success with novel-readers, because the characters too strictly reflected the moods of the author. But this trait helped his oratory.

a poor man to pay off debts which were not
legal debts nor debts of honor, but claims
upon business associates for whom he was not
strictly responsible, he was ever as ready to take
part in local political meetings as he was to
attend a State convention, and more ready to
read a sermon of Channing or Martineau to a
small flock of fellow-worshippers than he was
to put on the robes of a Chancellor of the University or to parade as a minister in foreign
courts. Enjoying every innocent pleasure to
the full—indeed, in our old Century Saturday
nights, remembering with Prince Hal, " the poor
creature, small beer," he was jovial with the
most jovial, knowing that pleasure builds up
and fortifies the nerves for the severer strains
of life; but he never went to excess, nor lost his
self-respect or dignity in any unseemly hilarity.
His absolute sincerity inspired a confidence as
absolute; and if circumstances compelled him
to break with an old friend, the rupture awak-
ened no resentments—only painful regrets that
it must be so.   He was only stern and unbend-
ing in the line of what he deemed his duty,
and even then,

" his wit, with fancy arm in arm,
Masked half its muscle in its skill to charm."

In a word, Mr. Curtis touched life at nearly every point at which it is possible for the individual soul to put forth its tendrils into the universe. As much as any landscape artist or poet he loved external Nature in all her moods and forms, her glancing lights and deepening shadows; he had the scholar's fondness for books, and could have lived forever in that magic world of truth and fiction which lies like a storage-battery on the shelves of every library; he delighted in pictures, of which he judged with a rare mastery without losing enthusiasm; he was enraptured by music, whether of the oratorio or the opera—of Jenny Lind or Paderewski or some humble St. Cecilia singing alone the touching melodies of the fireside; and yet he communed betimes with the "spiritual creatures who walk the earth, or when we wake or when we sleep," and often heard from steeps of echoing hills and thickets "celestial voices on the midnight air, sole or responsive to each other's song." One silver chord, it seems to me, bound his whole being in harmony. It was that innate, instinctive, spontaneous ideality which inspired, shaped, and toned his every feeling and thought as well as his every act. An aspiration for excellence, in its various forms of justice, truth, goodness, and courtesy, ever cast its light before his eyes and ever whispered in his ears, as the sea murmurs in the sea-shell of a vast Beyond which is its proper home.

It was this ideality which lured him as a boy to seek a golden age restored in the fraternity at Brook Farm; which led him to the neighborhood of Emerson and Hawthorne, and in after - life gathered around him so many noble friendships; which carried him to the sources of civilization in the mystic East, and to its splendid final achievements in Europe; which, with all his daintiness and reserve, made him so tolerant of uncouth and shambling reformers, in whose strident voices he heard the far-off preludes of coming harmonies; which opened a door from the severe labors of his every-day life into a dream-land of glorious hopes; which drew the sword of his eloquence against slavery and the unmanly degradations of our civic and political customs; which scattered so many jewels over his pages, and gave to his style at times the flavor of a luscious old wine, "with beaded bubbles winking at the brim," and

"Tasting of Flora and the country green,
  Dance, and Provençal song, and sun-burned mirth";

which accounts, too, for an occasional undertone of pensive sadness which escapes him, like the sigh of a strong man, and which made him profoundly religious—but with a religion that, defecated of the more acrid creeds, finds in the imperative law of Reverence for Manhood the highest, nay, the only conceivable, realization of an Eternal Love and Wisdom.

As I look back on this rare, sweet, gentle, great personality, there comes before me, as an external emblem of it, the palm-tree he once saw in Capri—gently throned upon a slope of richest green, and crowned with brilliant and fragrant flowers, as it rose in separate and peculiar stateliness in the odorous garden air. Towering far above its selected society of shining fig-trees and lustrous oleanders, it looked through the dream-mists of southern Italy down upon the bright bay of Naples, where all the civilizations of the ages have at some time passed—across to the islands of the sirens who sang to Ulysses; to the orange groves of Sorrento, where Tasso was born; and to the rocky shelves of Posilippo, where Virgil lies buried. As it looked, the birds came and lodged in its branches—tropic birds with their songs of love; birds of the far Norland, who chanted their mystic runes; and vocalists without a name, whose magic accents carry the secrets of the elves and fairies—while the people gathered in its shade for shelter, and ate its luscious fruit for strength, and listened to its melodies for cheer. But the palm, we are told, had a song of its own—a prophetic song, which told of a broad and ever-flowing river, ever flowing through greener grasses, under sunnier skies, to an eternal summer; typical of that grand stream of humanity which, though it sometimes breaks in cataracts, and bears the woes of earth on its bosom—funeral processions as well as festal processions—and reflects from its surface the storms no less than the smiles of heaven, is gliding ever on, ever on, to a future of larger liberty, surer justice, broader culture, and a universal love and peace. If that tree is now fallen, and its trunk lies prostrate on the mould that decays, and the birds sing no more in its branches, yet the echoes of its own song float on, and the thought of its beauty is to us who knew it, and will be to those who shall come to know it, "a joy forever"; yes, a joy forever—but

> "Oh for the touch of a vanished hand,
> And the sound of a voice that is still!"

At the close of Mr. Godwin's address Mr. Edmund C. Stedman rose to offer a motion, and said :

MR. PRESIDENT : A speaker whose voice is heard just after such an address realizes only too forcibly the pith of Armado's saying, "The words of Mercury are harsh after the songs of Apollo." None the less I would always feel remorse should I now forego the privilege of express-ing, however inadequately, what every one of this fit audi-ence, not few, desires to hear expressed. For we have all passed from interest to enjoyment, and from enjoyment to exaltation, under the spell of our veteran and noble eulo-gist. As the beauty of his tribute still haunts the ear, we reflect that but two of those whom the Century last year bore upon its rolls could have so moved us—the man to whom we have just listened, and the man whose life and attributes were his theme. The second has gone from us in his mellow prime ; the chance of time and fate has kindly left us the elder to declare the other's fame, and in the strength of age to supplement the records of his own dis-tinguished past and outvie the eloquence of younger men.

If there was much of felicity in the life of Curtis, he was not wholly bereft of it in his too early death. It is well with one who thus departs justified by such a tribute, and leaving a friend who, above all others, has the heart and the matchless natural gifts required for its utterance. And, in truth, who now is left of the silver-tongued group who spoke for us " in tears—in pleasure and in passion," save this our last of the orators ? His compeers have passed and are passing ; he sees a new generation about him, but not like that of which the Roman spoke, declaring that it is hard " to render an account before the men of a period different from that in which one has lived." For each of us would fain be his staff to-day, though we see he needs none. Long may it be the spirit of this Association to cherish to the utmost, to honor to the last, our sages, equipped with memory and wisdom, and uttering winged words, and still making its council-halls their home. The oration which has held our rapt attention is the latest, and second to no other, of our vouchers for the worth of this sweet tradition. There is not one of us who does not hold its pronouncer in gratitude and honor—not one who does not expect me to offer, as I now do, a resolution of thanks to Mr. Godwin for his beautiful and eloquent tribute to George William Curtis, and to make the request that he furnish the text of it for our distribution in printed form. Even that text, with all its lasting qualities, cannot wholly convey the strength of its delivery, for we all have noted how—as his mind caught fire by its own friction—he rose again and again above it with the fervor which only the impulse of the born orator can display.

Mr. Stedman's resolution, seconded by Henry Howland and others, was unanimously adopted.

9

THE END.

www.ingramcontent.com/pod-product-compliance
Lightning Source LLC
Chambersburg PA
CBHW030027030726
47499CB00008B/3149